RUSTY ROCKS!

W9-BIN-857

BY **MARY TILLWORTH**

BASED ON THE TELEPLAY "RUSTY ROCKS" BY SUZANNE BOLCH AND JOHN MAY

ILLUSTRATED BY **DAVE AIKINS**

A Random House PICTUREBACK® Book
Random House 🏠 New York

randomhousekids.com
ISBN 978-1-5247-1721-6
Printed in the United States of America
10 9 8 7 6 5 4 3 2 1

One morning, Rusty was working on a new project with his robotic dino, Botasaur, and his mini robot helpers, the Bits.

"This stage is really coming together!" Rusty said as he bolted the last spotlight into place. "Awesome teamwork, everybody!"

Rusty's friend Ruby drove up in her buggy. She gasped when she saw what they had made.

"No way!" she said. "Is this part of the stage for the Sparkton Hills Talent Show?"

Rusty smiled. "Yep."

"What are you going to do for your act?" Ruby asked.

"Let's get the stage to the park, and I'll show you!" Rusty said.

After the team took the stage apart and loaded the pieces onto the trailer attached to Rusty's go-kart, he hopped in, put on his helmet, and started up the engine. "Time to bolt!" he said.

Rusty and Ruby zoomed through the streets with Botasaur and the Bits following close behind.

At the park, Rusty, Botasaur, and the Bits reassembled the stage. Chef Betty came over. "What are you going to do in the show to dazzle us?"

"Botasaur and I are doing pet tricks!" Rusty jumped onto the end of Botasaur's tail, and the dino robot tossed him high into the air.

Rusty flipped over the dino's head and then slid down the length of his tail.

"Ooh! Ah! Ooh!" Rusty said, rubbing his bottom. "The last part is a bumpy ride, but we're working on it."

"What about you, Ruby?" Chef Betty asked.

"I'm going to sing." Ruby cleared her throat. *"Laaa . . ."* Her voice trailed off. She sighed. "Sorry. When I try to sing, my tummy gets all tingly."

"I know what's wrong," said Rusty. "You just need a microphone!" He grabbed his Multitool and used it to build one from spare parts. When he was finished, he announced, "Introducing . . . Ruby Ramirez!"

Ruby gulped when she saw people in the park staring at her.
"I sing all the time," she said, "but onstage, it's kinda . . . scary."
"Aww, it sounds like you have stage fright," said Chef Betty.
"The talent show is starting soon. What am I going to do?" Ruby moaned.

Rusty and Ruby went over to the swing set to think.

"Let's see," said Ruby. "What's something else I'm *really* good at that won't be scary to do onstage?"

"I know!" replied Rusty. "Dancing! You've been taking lessons since forever!"

Ruby stood up and broke out some moves. She was awesome!

Then Ruby saw some kids watching her. "Wow!" one of them said. Ruby immediately stumbled and tripped over her own feet.

"Well, I'm good at tumbling all over the place," she said sheepishly. "Too bad that couldn't be my act."

"Maybe it can! What if you did a gymnastics routine?" Rusty and Ruby went to the soccer goal. "Show us what you can do!" he said to his friend.

"Here goes!" Ruby flipped and spun around the bar. She was incredible!

But when Ruby realized she had an audience, she lost her grip and fell to the ground.

"I still have that feeling in my tummy. I can't stop freezing up whenever people watch me perform," she said sadly.

Botasaur and the Bits gathered around Ruby and snuggled her.
"Aww. You guys make me feel so much better," she told them.
"I could do anything with you around."

Rusty snapped his fingers. "That's it! Ruby gets nervous when she performs alone. Maybe she doesn't have to. Let's combine it and design it!"

Rusty raced back to the Rivet Lab. He hauled out cans, hubcaps, bars, and pipes. With the Bits by his side, Rusty drilled, hammered, and spray-painted away.

Rusty took his invention back to the park. With a big *thunk*, he put the final touch on a super-cool rock-band kit.

"Modified, customized, Rustified—the instruments for Ruby and the Rustettes!" he announced proudly.

Ruby gasped. "You did this for me?"

Rusty nodded. "Of course! You won't feel so nervous onstage if we're all up there with you."

Ruby grinned. "Thanks, Rusty!"

Night fell, and it was time for the talent show! Ruby and Rusty watched act after act, including an amazing performance by an opera-singing monkey.

After the monkey bowed, Chef Betty called to them, "You're up next!"

Ruby took the stage with Rusty and the Bits. She looked at Rusty and smiled. She was ready!

"Hello, Sparkton Hills!" she said into her microphone. Then she took a deep breath and began to sing. With her friends by her side, she wasn't scared at all. Under the bright spotlights, Ruby and the Rustettes rocked out!

At the end of the talent show, Chef Betty gave the crowd the news they'd all been waiting for.

"The winner of the Sparkton Hills Talent Show is . . . Kiki, the opera-singing monkey! And second prize goes to . . . Ruby and the Rustettes!"

Ruby and the Rustettes climbed the stage and took a bow in front of the cheering audience.

Ruby hugged Rusty and the Bits. "I want to say thanks to my friends. We rocked it together!"

© Spin Master Ltd.

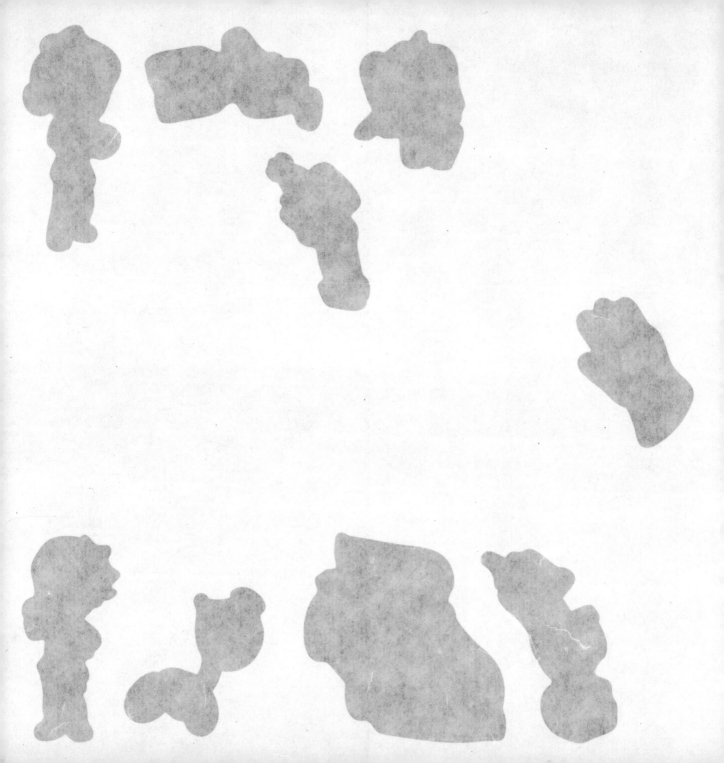